Rock and Roll
Divas Supreme

Robin Epstein

Scholastic Inc.

New York Toronto London Auckland Sydney
Mexico City New Delhi Hong Kong Buenos Aires

Read all the books about the Groovy Girls!

To Maddie, Benjy, and Eli,
my inspiration!

Cover illustration by Taia Morley
Interior illustrations by Yancey Labat

ISBN 0-439-81434-0

12 11 10 9 8 7 6 5 4 3 2   5 6 7 8 9 10/0

Printed in the U.S.A.
First Little Apple printing, September 2005

WARBINEK

Chapter 1

Musical Chairs

MUSIC CLOSET

"**S**o, do you think I look like a tuba?" Reese asked her best friend, Gwen. "Or would you say I'm more of a bassoon?"

"To be honest," Gwen replied, as they walked into music class, "I think you're more of a French horn!"

"A French horn?" Reese asked, thinking about the curvy brass instrument. "Am I happy about that?"

"*Oui, oui!* It's classy, it's sassy, and it's Frenchy,"

French Horn

Gwen replied. "Take it from a girl who looks like a cello." Gwen bowed out her knees to demonstrate. With her legs in that position, she *did* resemble the oversized violin.

Cello

But Reese and Gwen weren't the only ones trying to figure out the instruments that fit them.

Everyone in music class was abuzz because today was musical instrument assignment day!

"How do you think Mr. Hornblower will decide who gets which instrument?" Oki asked O'Ryan.

"Beats me," O'Ryan replied. "Hey—maybe I should play the bongos!" She pounded her chest Tarzan-style to prove her point.

"Definitely." Oki laughed. "You're completely bongos! You think he might give me a harp?"

Harp

"You? A harp? I don't think so. I mean, don't you have to be an angel or something to play one of those?" O'Ryan asked.

"Well, I don't know if I'm an angel," Oki said. "But I *do* like the idea of harp music playing behind me whenever I make an entrance!"

"Ca-lasssss!" Mr. Hornblower said, as he walked in the room. "As I'm sure you know, getting an instrument is a very important moment in one's life."

Mr. Hornblower was a man born to be a music teacher. Not only did he have the perfect last name for the job, but his nose was shaped like a clarinet!

As he twittered on about the meaning of music and the importance of each instrument, no one was really paying attention.

"I wish he'd just stop and let us know what we're gonna get already," Gwen whispered to Reese.

"Oki!" Mr. Hornblower called out.

"Mr. Hornblower!" Oki replied.

"Let's take a walk to the instrument closet, shall we?"

"*Zuper!*" Oki said, jumping out of her seat and skipping to the back of the room.

When the door to the instrument shelves swung open, the whole class OOOOOOOHHED! The closet was filled with every musical instrument you could think of—and a few you'd probably never heard of, like the bonang, a Javanese kettle gong, and the kalimba, an African thumb piano!

"Groovy!" Oki said, as she peered in.

Mr. Hornblower smiled. "Now, Oki, many people consider the instrument you'll be playing to be the voice of jazz. Can you guess what it is?"

"Not the harp, right?" Oki asked.

"No!" Mr. Hornblower tut-tutted. "But I'll give you a hint. This instrument is also played by John Coltrane, President Bill Clinton, and Lisa Simpson."

Saxophone

Oki's face lit up. "The saxophone?"

Her teacher nodded.

"That's perfect," O'Ryan yelled. "'Cause Oki's the jazziest girl in class!"

Trumpet

"O'Ryan McCloud," Mr. Hornblower said, waving her back, "you're next. I had to think long and hard about what instrument suited you, and then it came to me—the trumpet—'cause I think you're a girl who likes to sound off!"

"Well, that makes dollars-and-sense," Reese said. "And O'Ryan *is* always blowing hot air!"

"Ha-ha," O'Ryan replied, taking hold of the trumpet. "And I can't wait to blow it every morning to wake you up!"

"Okay, Gwen," Mr. Hornblower said. "Now, you've always struck me as a girl who would know what to do with a pair of drumsticks."

"You betcha!" Gwen answered. "I love drumsticks—and chicken wings, too!" She laughed, running toward the music closet and grabbing hold of two wooden sticks. She drummed them in the air, making all the appropriate drum noises with her mouth.

"Mike?" Mr. Hornblower said.

Mike didn't respond right away. He was too busy shuffling a deck of cards under his desk.

"Yo, Earth to space boy!" Gwen said, tapping her drumsticks against Mike's desk.

"Sorry, Mr. Hornblower," Mike answered, flicking a card at Gwen as he stood up. Mike had been practicing his card tricks a lot lately, so the chucked card gave a perfect karate chop to Gwen's knee.

"Ow!" Gwen howled.

"Ow!" Mike mimicked.

"Well, Mike, I hope you and Gwen are going to get along better than that," Mr. Hornblower said, pulling out another pair of drumsticks. "Because, I've also assigned you to the drums."

"Are you kidding?" Mike asked.

"Because that's not very funny, Mr. Hornblower," Gwen replied, finishing Mike's sentence.

Mike walked over to the instrument closet and took his set of drumsticks from the teacher.

Snare Drums and Cymbals

"No, I'm not joking," Mr. Hornblower replied. "So you two will just have to learn to work with each other. There are two snare drums back there. I'm sure you'll be making beautiful music together in no time!"

Both Gwen and Mike rolled their eyes.

"See that?" Mr. Hornblower said. "Simpatico already. Now, Reese!"

Reese nodded and started for the back of the room, ready to receive her *chi-chi* French horn.

"You pay great attention to detail, and you're also very sensitive," Mr. Hornblower said. "So I think you'll have an amazing aptitude for your instrument."

With the mention of the word "aptitude," Reese got a bad feeling. She didn't exactly know that it meant "natural ability," but what she *did* know was that whenever anyone used that word, it always seemed to mean you had to work hard.

When Reese reached the instrument closet, Mr. Hornblower handed her a violin case. "I think you have the potential to be a real prodigy," Mr. Hornblower said. "You know, someone who, though young, is still able to do something like a great master!"

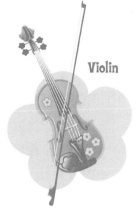

Violin

"Really?" Reese asked, flattered by the compliment and taking the instrument out of its case.

When Mr. Hornblower finished handing out all the instruments, he gave a quick lesson to each student, showing everyone how to handle and play their new sound-making machines!

"This is *so* way fun!" Gwen exclaimed, holding tight to her drumsticks as if they were attached to her hands. "Rat-tat-tat-tat-tat," she said, as she rolled the sticks against the snare drum.

"Good!" Mr. Hornblower said. "And now that you all 'know' how to play, I think you're ready to perform a little concert, right?"

"Yeah!" O'Ryan said.

"Totally!" Oki yelled, gripping her sax.

"*Bravissimo!*" Mr. Hornblower replied, knowing full well that no one would really be able to play any music at this point. "So, on my count, I want you to begin playing an easy tune that you all know: 'Row, Row, Row Your Boat.' Okay, and a

One-E and a Two-E and a Three!" He nodded to the class, raised his arms, and began to conduct his new musicians.

SQUEEEEEEAKKKKKKKKK!
HOOOOONNNNKKKKKKK!
CRASH-BING-BANG!
BOOM!

The song sounded *nothing* like "Row, Row, Row Your Boat."

But nobody seemed to mind—or even be aware of—the awful sound. Because to them, more than anything else, it sounded like everyone was having a blast!

Chapter 2

Making the (Hair) Band

"**Y**ou look like a chipmunk!" Reese giggled at O'Ryan. "Like you're storing nuts in your cheeks for winter." The girls were camped out at their mom's vintage clothing store, "Hey, Betty," after school that day.

"I do not!" O'Ryan replied defensively. "This is how I'm *supposed* to practice my trumpet." She puffed air in and out of her cheeks and blew into the mouthpiece.

PPPPPPPPPFFFFFFFFFFTTTTTTTTTT, the trumpet wailed.

"Pfft, yourself!" Reese said. "You *still* look like a chipmunk."

"Well, you look like a hedgehog!" O'Ryan replied.

Okay, O'Ryan didn't *really* think Reese looked like a hedgehog—but she was getting frustrated. She still hadn't been able to produce any good sounds from her trumpet, no matter how hard she tried.

And what was worse: Reese was right! O'Ryan *did* look a lot like a chipmunk when she played. A chipmunk whose face was turning a brighter and brighter red with each huff and puff! O'Ryan took another big breath.

Ppppffffffffffffaaaaaaa, the trumpet tooted lamely.

"Uh, O'Ryan," Mom said, waving her hands and running up to the front of the store where the twins were sitting. "I love that you want to practice your new instrument, but I don't think my store is the best place to do it."

"Why not?" O'Ryan asked.

"Because you'll scare away the customers!" Reese replied.

Just as O'Ryan was about to inform her twin that it wasn't her trumpet-playing, but the sound of her sister's voice that would scare the customers, the bell above the store's door jingled.

"Well, fancy seeing you dude-ettes!" Yvette said, as she and Vanessa walked in.

"Hey, guys! What brings you to 'Hey, Betty'?" Reese asked, happily surprised by her friends' visit.

"We're here to find costumes," Vanessa replied.

"Costumes?" O'Ryan asked. "For what?"

"Well," said Yvette, leaning in, "we were chatting with our teacher after class..." She let this info hang there for a moment so the twins understood how special this was. "And she told us—*confidentially*—that tomorrow they'll be making an announcement about the school talent show."

"There's going to be a talent show?" Reese repeated excitedly.

"Ssshhhh! Keep it down," Vanessa said. "We don't want the whole world to know about it just yet. But, yeah. There's gonna be a talent show in a few weeks."

"And that's why we're here now. We want to

get a jump on getting our outfits together," Yvette added.

"Good thinking!" O'Ryan whispered, genuinely impressed. "So what are you guys planning to do?"

"I'm going to *sing*!" Yvette replied, singing the word "sing."

"You, too?" Reese asked Vanessa.

Vanessa shook her head. "No way!" she replied. "I mean, I know I'm amazing at a lot of things, but singing is not one of them. I'll be doing something I'm truly talented at instead: directing."

"That's right!" Yvette said. "Vanessa is my manager, director, and guru all rolled into one."

"Oooh!" Vanessa said, her eye catching the glimmer of a spangled gown. "And the guru thinks this would be a very hot little number for you to wear!" She pulled the gown off a pile of clothes and held it against Yvette. "What do you think?"

"Uh," Yvette said, wrinkling her nose, "I guess I was thinking something a little more jazzy. You know, snug-fitting and belly-baring!"

"Forget it!" Vanessa replied, shaking her head. "Bellies are so last year."

"Can you give us a little preview of what you're gonna sing?" Reese asked Yvette, switching the talk back to the talent part of the show.

"Yeah," O'Ryan pleaded. "Give your fans a little somethin'!"

"I don't know—" Yvette replied.

"Go ahead, Yvette, give them a little taste," Vanessa said. "It'll be good practice."

"Well, if my director says it's okay!" Yvette replied. "I'll sing a little ditty from one of my favorite bands, The Randoms. You know The Randoms—they're the group with lyrics as odd and off-the-wall as their hairdos. Okay, ready?"

Yvette curled her fingers around an invisible microphone and held it up to her mouth. Then she closed her eyes and said, "This one goes out to the grooviest girls I know."

> *"Purple T-shirt, red socks*
> *Yellow taxis on the block,*
> *These are things I like a lot*
> *Jumping rope makes me hot!"*

Yvette strode back and forth across her "stage" and kept singing the random Randoms' lyrics to the delight of everyone in the store. And when she got to the final verse, she belted out:

> *"And I don't know if you'll get me*
> *But I don't care, don't you see?*
> *So listen up and let it be*
> *'Cause the music it will set us free!"*

As soon as Yvette finished the song, all the girls—and everyone else in the store—applauded wildly. Yvette took a bow and beamed.

"Can my girl sing or what?" Vanessa said, throwing an arm around Yvette.

"She's a-mazing, grace!" O'Ryan replied.

"Supreme, like a member of the Supremes!" Reese said.

"The Supremes?" Vanessa asked. "Who are they?"

"Ya don't know?" Reese replied. "They're only, like, the first and best girl group ever!"

"That's right," Yvette said, and turned to Mrs. McCloud. "They were popular way back when you were a girl, right?"

"Right," Mrs. McCloud said with a laugh. "And just for the record, it wasn't really *that* long ago."

"Anyway," Reese continued, "the Supremes totally rocked."

"So what happened to them?" Vanessa asked.

"They 'Stopped, in the Name of Love,'" Yvette sang, belting out a play on a verse from one of the group's most popular songs.

"Yeah, it was pretty tragic," Reese said. "The lead singer decided to go solo, and it broke up the group."

"Maybe you should sing one of their songs, Yvette," O'Ryan suggested.

"OMG, wait!" Yvette shouted. "I just got an even *better* idea. What if we formed a group and played together in the talent show like the Supremes? I would be the lead singer, and you guys could be my band!"

O'Ryan's eyes widened. "That'd be super-fly!" she replied, blowing into her trumpet as if adding another exclamation point to the thought.

"O'Ryan," Reese said, shaking her head at her sister. "We just got our instruments today. How are we supposed to be able to play them well enough for a talent show in a few weeks?"

"Well, I *know* we're not ready yet. But if we put our minds to it, I'm sure we'll be good enough by then," O'Ryan replied. "And anyway," she added, teasing Reese, "you're supposed to be the big 'prodigy,' aren't you?"

Vanessa put her hands on her hips and thought about the idea for a moment herself. On the one hand, Reese had a point. It was hard to imagine the girls would be good enough to play in a few weeks. But, on the other hand, Vanessa realized that if directing Yvette alone was already this much fun, being able to direct *all* the Groovy Girls in a band would be five times more fun!

"You know what?" Vanessa said, beginning to move the girls into place as if they were already onstage. "We should do this! I'm seeing matching costumes, matching hair bands, matching accessories! Oh, man, the Groovy Group will rock steady!"

"We'll rock and roll!" O'Ryan said.

"We'll rock out!" Yvette added.

"C'mon, Reese, what do you say?" Vanessa asked.

Reese looked at her friends, and she could only think of one thing—if any group of girls could do it, it would be the Groovies. Reese nodded her head. "I say, okay, and look out school, 'cause the Groovy Group will be supreme!"

And as the girls hugged on it, little did they know exactly how "supreme"—or not—they were about to be.

Chapter 3

Give It a Rest!

"**Y**ou can tell me—and be honest," O'Ryan said to her puppy. "Do I blow *at* the trumpet?"

"AARRRUUUUUUU!" little Sleepless howled in response. He looked at O'Ryan with sad puppy eyes and wagged his tail.

"You're right, I stink!" O'Ryan replied, flinging herself on her bed.

She'd been practicing her trumpet for what seemed like hours every day since she'd gotten it.

Yet, still…she stank.

"But maybe if I just practice a little more, I'll get it," O'Ryan said, recovering quickly and refusing to give up.

"AARRRRUUUU!" Sleepless cried again.

"Good, glad you agree!" O'Ryan smiled and bent down to kiss the puppy on his head.

AARRRUUU!!!

"Maybe he's whimpering because he wants you to *stop* playing!" Reese said as she entered the twins' bedroom. "Did you ever think of that?"

The dog looked up at Reese and again wagged his tail. (It was as if he understood what she had just said, Reese thought—and agreed with her!)

"Well, *excuse* me for trying to improve myself!" O'Ryan replied, scolding both her sister and the dog. "The trumpet—unlike your violin—happens to be a very hard instrument to play!"

"Hey, the violin's no walk in the park, either," Reese said. "I just happen to be a *prodigy*." She smiled smugly at her sister.

To prove it, Reese picked up her violin and played a very fast and mostly excellent version of

"Twinkle, Twinkle Little Star." When she was finished, she bowed deeply, just to rub it in.

But O'Ryan didn't applaud. "Let me try it," she said instead, reaching for the violin. She was hoping that if Reese could play the violin well, she would be able to do so, too.

"Sure," Reese said. "Here ya go."

Reese handed O'Ryan the violin and watched as her sister awkwardly tried to balance it on her shoulder. "No, like this," Reese instructed, showing O'Ryan how to tuck the violin under her chin.

"Oh, right," O'Ryan said. She took the bow and ran it back and forth across the strings, fully expecting to hear "Twinkle, Twinkle Little Star."

SCREEEEEEECCCCHHHH! the strings shrieked.

"Aaaah!" Reese yelled, putting her hands over her ears.

"Why is it making that noise?" O'Ryan said, moving the bow again.

SCREEEEEEECCCCCHHHH! the instrument cried again.

"Stop!" Reese shouted.

"What did you do to the violin to make it sound good?" O'Ryan asked.

"Nothing special, I swear!" Reese said. "You just saw me play it. Here, give it back."

Reese took the violin back from O'Ryan and started playing it again. This time she breezed through a version of "Sunrise, Sunset."

What the heck was going on here?

Why is all this music stuff coming so easily to Reese and not to me? O'Ryan wondered.

Reese hadn't practiced her violin for nearly as much time as O'Ryan had spent playing her trumpet. Yet, here was Reese, playing songs on her violin that actually sounded like...songs! And O'Ryan was still only making sounds come out of her trumpet that sounded like, well...burps!

O'Ryan picked up her trumpet. "Excuse me," she said, turning away from her sister. "But I need to get back to practicing."

"Don't you think it's time to give it a rest?"

Reese asked O'Ryan. "And I'm not just talking about the rests written into the music."

"I just need to spend a little more time on it," O'Ryan responded. "Then I'm sure it'll come to me."

Reese shook her head. "It doesn't always work that way, you know."

O'Ryan narrowed her eyes at her twin, the *prodigy*. "Oh, now I get it!" she said.

"Get what?" Reese asked.

"I know why you want me to stop practicing."

"Huh?" Reese replied.

"You don't want me to get any better at the trumpet because you like the idea that you're better at something than me!"

"O'Ryan, that's nuts!" Reese replied.

"Is it?" O'Ryan asked, pointing her index finger at her sister.

The idea had never occurred to Reese before. But when she thought about it, maybe it *did* make a little sense. After all, O'Ryan had *always* been much better than her at soccer. And though she hadn't spent much  time thinking about it, every now and again Reese *did* think it might be nice to be better than her sister at something.

So maybe—just maybe—without even *realizing* it, Reese *had* been enjoying the fact that she was much better at musical things than her seven-minutes-older sister!

"You know what? You're full of baloney," Reese said.

"Well, you won't mind if I keep practicing, then?" O'Ryan said loudly.

"I think you should!" Reese replied with just as much emphasis. "And I'll practice my violin."

"Good!"

So both girls picked up their instruments and played as loudly as they could, in an attempt to drown each other out.

...Which lasted for about thirty seconds.

"GIRLS!" Mom said, waving her arms as she

entered their bedroom. "What's going on here?"

"We're practicing," the twins said together.

"Really?" Mom replied. "Because it sounded like you were trying to wake up sleeping children in China!"

"Sorry, Mom," O'Ryan said.

"Yeah, we'll try to keep it down from now on," Reese added.

"Well," Mom said, softening. "I assume, if you're practicing, that you've finished up all your homework?"

"Uh," said Reese.

"Um," added O'Ryan.

"So I take that as a 'no, Mom, we haven't'?" The twins nodded.

"Okay, then. So the instruments go away until the homework is complete. You can practice more when you're done if you want," Mom said. "Deal?"

The girls nodded again.

"Thank you, ladies," Mom said as she started walking out the door. "I'll be looking forward to your next concert—a little later and a lot less loud."

The twins actually had a lot of homework left to do. But thankfully, it was in English and Math—O'Ryan and Reese's specialties.

"So you'll do the Math assignment first, right?"

O'Ryan asked Reese.

"Yup," Reese replied. "And you'll do the English assignment?"

O'Ryan nodded. "And then we'll check each other's work?"

"Of course," Reese said. "Just like always."

And just like always, Reese, who was stronger in Math, and O'Ryan, who was stronger in English, came to each other's rescue. After all, despite the differences in their musical-instrument-playing abilities, sometimes having a sister who was better than you at something could be a very good thing!

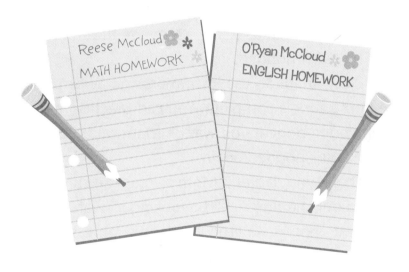

Chapter 4
Getting Into a Jam

"Wait a minute!" Reese said, as the girls set up for their rehearsal in the McClouds' garage.

"What's the prob?" Vanessa replied, looking up from her clipboard.

"What am I going to do?" Reese asked.

"What do you mean?"

"I mean," Reese said, "I was just thinking— rock bands don't have violin players."

All the Groovies stopped in their disco tracks and turned to Reese. No one had thought about that little detail until right this very minute.

"Holy tuba toothpaste!" Gwen exclaimed. "She's totally right!"

O'Ryan couldn't help it—this problem seemed kind of funny to her. (She felt like it was the first time she'd smiled since getting her miserable trumpet.) "Wow, that's too bad," she said. "I mean, it's a real shame you're a violin prodigy, instead of being good at something more rockin' like Dad's guitar."

O'Ryan motioned to Dad's old bass guitar in the corner of the garage. Their dad had told the girls many a time that he used to play the guitar "back in the day"—and he had taught the girls a few bass lines.

"That's *it*!" Vanessa shouted excitedly. "Reese can play the bass instead of the violin. Every rock band worth its sound system has a bass player!"

"Good thought," Reese said. "But there's only one problem: I only know three lines."

"Okay, well, I know it's not exactly like the violin," Vanessa replied. "But work with me here. It's the same idea with the strings and stuff, right?"

"It's worth a shot, I guess." Reese took the guitar out of its case and hooked its strap around her back.

And sure enough, starting with her three bass lines, Reese plucked something that almost sounded like music! (Mr. Hornblower had been right: Reese really *was* gifted!)

"Rock and roll, Reese! You sound awwwesome," Vanessa said proudly. "So okay, girls, let's get practicing."

"But we haven't picked a song yet," Yvette reminded her.

"Yes, we have," Vanessa said confidently. "Or at least, I should say, *I* have. You're going to be playing 'Chick-a-Chick-a-Cha-Cha.'"

Vanessa's Clipboard

✓ Chick-a-
Chick-a-
Cha-Cha

"Why do *you* get to decide what song we do?" Gwen asked.

"Because I'm the artistic director and that's what artistic directors do," Vanessa replied. Then she nodded, as if daring anyone to doubt her. "Here, listen to it on my iPod. You'll love it."

Vanessa connected her music player to the mini-speakers she'd brought along, and turned the song on full volume.

"Oh baby, yoooooooouuuuuuuuuu,
You are my morning breeze
You solve my mysteries
You cure my heart disease."

Oki's foot started tapping to the beat. Gwen's head bounced back and forth, and O'Ryan and Reese were swaying. And when the chorus came around for the second time, Yvette started singing, too.

"Chick-a-chick-a-cha-cha
Chick-a-chick-a-cha-cha
Chick-a-chick-a-cha-cha-cha!"

The girls all looked around at one another.

Vanessa was right! This was definitely the song they should be playing for the talent show.

When the song was over, Yvette high-fived Vanessa.

"You're the best artistic director I've ever had," Yvette said.

"Thanks," Vanessa replied. "Although I'm probably also the *only* one you've ever had! Which reminds me: I've already

scheduled another rehearsal—a sleepover—for this weekend. Cool with everyone?"

The Groovies thought that was a great idea.

"Okay, good. Now girls, please take your positions!"

All the girls in the Groovy Group went to their instruments, with everyone standing just behind and to the side of their lead singer, ready to jam.

Reese tightened the strap on her bass.

Oki picked up her sax.

O'Ryan started puffing out her cheeks and did the fingering on her trumpet's buttons.

And Gwen got behind her set of makeshift drums, which, for today, were really just a large set of plastic pails and tin cans.

"I'll keep the song playing and you girls just jump in and play what you can on your instruments," Vanessa instructed. "And here, Yvette," she said, handing her a copy of the lyrics.

"Okay, let's rock!" Yvette replied, glancing over the words to the song.

When Vanessa pushed play on the iPod, the music started.

But when the other girls started playing, well, that's when it stopped sounding like music and started sounding more like *mu-SICK*!

Yvette was singing beautifully. But you could barely hear her because the sound of her voice was being drowned out by the terrible noise!

So she tried singing louder.

Nothing.

She tried yelling the words.

Still nothing.

Then she began shouting.

"Stop playing so loud and so bad!"

(Actually, Reese sounded pretty okay, but you couldn't really tell because of the way the others were playing.)

But the other girls kept playing because, well, *no one could hear Yvette telling them not to*!

But this wasn't fun or funny to Yvette. She thought the Groovy Group was a disaster!

And she thought the girls were exactly the opposite of supreme.

Finally, she thought, *I'm totally out of here!* Balling her hands into fists, she yelled, "I CAN'T WORK LIKE THIS!"

But, of course, since everyone was playing so loudly, no one heard that, either.

Instead, they just saw Yvette as she stormed out of the garage. And the only hint of an explanation that they got was the word **Diva!** printed in pretty pink script on the back of her T-shirt.

Chapter 5

The Morning After the Day Before

"Totally! Good idea! You should definitely do a solo," Vanessa said to Yvette the next A.M. at school, agreeing with the suggestion her friend had just made.

Feathers had been ruffled at yesterday's band practice (Yvette feathers). And Vanessa knew that the Groovy Group's star singer needed some soothing.

"Thank you," Yvette replied, as she brushed her

hair in the bathroom mirror. "I was hoping you'd understand."

"I do. And I want you to feel confident that, as director, I'll do everything I can to make the band's practices go better from now on," Vanessa added.

Yvette stopped fixing her hair, and turned to Vanessa. "I don't think you get what I mean."

Vanessa put her hand up. "Oh, I completely get it, Yvette, I do. Look-it!" She took her clipboard out of her backpack. And with her special artistic director pen, she wrote in all caps: YVETTE SINGS A SOLO!!!

When Vanessa finished writing this, she was very pleased with herself. "So, which part do you want to sing by yourself?" she asked Yvette. "The Chick-a-Chick-a chorus, the opening, or what? "

Yvette shook her head. "Here's the deal: I want to sing all by myself. Completely. No backup band. Get it?"

"Yvette, it'll all work out fabulously, you'll see! I mean, right now the Groovy Group *does* sound pretty ugly. And I understand why you wouldn't want to have a bad backup band." Vanessa smiled with all of her teeth. "That's why the girls will practice even harder now, so there's no chance they'll embarrass you!"

"No go!" Yvette responded.

"But Yvette," Vanessa tried again. "You're our lead singer! And without you, the band would be... would be...it would be...nothing."

Yvette looked down. "Yeah," she said, "I really *do* feel bad about that."

"But you were the one who said we should form a group in the first place!" Vanessa pleaded.

"I know," Yvette said. "But *you* could still be my artistic director."

Vanessa thought about this idea for a moment. But where would this leave the other girls? *Nowheresville*!

"FRIENDS DO <u>NOT</u> DO THIS TO ONE ANOTHER! HOW CAN YOU DO THIS TO <u>US</u>?" Vanessa said really loudly.

"I'm sorry," Yvette replied. "But still, what am I s'posed to do? I mean, I really want to win."

"Well, who says we can't win without you?" Vanessa said, suddenly changing her tune. "'Cause when the school gets a load of my Groovy Girls up onstage, it's going to be all razzle-dazzle, see?"

Then, in what was almost a repeat performance of the day before, Vanessa balled up her fists just like Yvette had done yesterday in the twins' garage, and she stormed out of the girls' bathroom.

But as she strode down the hall, Vanessa realized all her big talk didn't change the fact that now the Groovy Group was short a lead singer.

And without a singer, who would lead the audience in chicka-chicka and cha-cha-cha-ing?

"Hey, Vanessa!" O'Ryan called out to her as she was about to walk past the other girls without even seeing them.

"Oh, hi, chickies," Vanessa replied.

"What's wrong?" Reese asked, seeing that their

normally rah-rah leader was slinking with a slump.

"News-flash," Vanessa said. "We no longer have a lead singer! And even though I told Yvette I *thought* we'd be able to win the talent show without her, just between us, I think we might be sunk!"

The Groovies let this info sink in for a moment.

"Wait a minute!" Oki finally said. "What about that group the 'Hot 'n' Sweaties'?"

"What about them?" Reese asked.

"Well, during their concerts they do a lot of hopping and bopping around the stage, right?"

"Which is why they get hot 'n' sweaty!" Gwen replied.

"I heard that sometimes they lip-synch their songs— you know, mouthing the words to the music during a concert—so they can do the dance moves without sounding all breathless," Oki added.

O'Ryan looked at her best friend. "Oki, if you're thinking what I'm thinking you're thinking, I'm thinking you're brilliant!"

"Thank you," Oki replied.

It took the other girls a minute to catch up, but soon enough, they all caught Oki's drift.

"We can lip-synch. Of course!" Vanessa exclaimed. "That's a great idea!"

"So does this mean the Groovy Group is back in action?" Reese asked.

"You bet it does," Vanessa said, perking up. "And we're gonna be better than ever! So from now till the time of the talent show next week, we're gonna practice 24/7!"

This was intense. But this was also exciting.

"And," Vanessa continued, "that sleepover we were planning to have this weekend? Well, it's going to be all about making our band supreme."

And as the Groovies headed into class, they realized their talent extended way beyond their musical abilities (which was a good thing!). Because now they all knew they weren't just four fearless musical instrument players (and one artistic director). They were amazingly creative problem solvers, too!

Chapter 6

Practice Makes Perfect?

"Can I help you guys carry anything inside?" Vanessa asked the twins the evening of the sleepover. She'd arrived early, just as the girls were unloading the slumber party goodies from the car.

"That's okay," Reese said, "the pretzels, popcorn, and nacho chips don't weigh too much."

"Until I eat them," Mr. McCloud said, laughing. "And *then* I swear each one weighs at least a pound!"

Once inside, Vanessa took out her clipboard and showed the girls the multi-colored rehearsal schedule she'd made.

"Wow," Reese said, looking over the detailed chart. "It doesn't even look like we'll have time to eat!"

"Sure we will," Vanessa replied. "See? Says right here: REHEARSE. REHEARSE. REHEARSE. REHEARSE SOME MORE. TALK ABOUT COSTUMES. REHEARSE. PIZZA. BED."

"Did I hear someone mention pizza?" Gwen asked, knocking on the door and joining the party.

"We were just going over our practice schedule," Reese explained. "And Vanessa made 'pizza time' right before 'bedtime.'"

"I'm not sure having pizza right before bed is such a good idea," Gwen said.

"'Cause eating right before you go to bed will give you funny dreams?" O'Ryan asked.

"No, 'cause I don't think I can wait that long to have my extra-cheesy delight! Matter of fact, I'm feeling a little hungry-hungry-hippo-ish right now!"

"Okay," Vanessa replied, taking up her clipboard

and writing a note to herself: Feed Gwen!!!

"A little help with the door, please!" Oki shouted from outside.

"Hiya, Oki," O'Ryan said, opening the door for her best friend.

"Hola," Oki answered, as she struggled with several large bags and her sax. "Lookie, ladies! I brought some stuff for the party."

"Presents for us?" Reese smiled, pointing to the shopping bags.

"Oki, you shouldn't have! But I'm oh-so-glad you did!" O'Ryan laughed.

"Sorry to say these *aren't* gifts for my fave fraternal twins." Oki smiled. "But they *are* for the Groovy Group! I raided my mom's closet for some things that we might be able to wear onstage."

Before the girls had the chance to inspect Oki's treasures, there was another knock at the door.

It was Yvette. The *former* lead singer of the Groovy Group.

"Hey, Yvette, glad you could make it!" Reese said.

"Hi, everyone," Yvette said, giving a small wave to the other girls. She looked a little nervous—like she didn't know if she was really welcome.

Of course, Yvette *had* been invited to the slumber party—she was still an official member of the Groovy Girls. But...ever since she told Vanessa she didn't want to sing with the Groovy Group, things were a little tricky-icky between them. And Yvette didn't know if the other girls would be so happy to have her at their rehearsal sleepover.

Yet Groovy Girls are groovy for a reason, and one of those reasons is that they're amazingly understanding friends. So, true to their groovitude, all the girls made Yvette feel welcome.

"You know we're going to be rehearsing during the whole sleepover, right?" Vanessa said.

(Well, *almost all* the girls made her feel welcome.)

"Yeah, I know," Yvette said. "I'll just hang out and rehearse on my own."

"Okay," Vanessa replied. "But don't go trying

to steal any of our moves!" Then she paused. "Just kidding!" And she laughed. "Not like we even *have* any moves you'd want to steal! And, by the way, about this whole singing-on-your-own thing, I get it and, you know, I love ya, anyway."

"Beautilicious!" Yvette smiled. She was very happy things had been patched up. (The idea that her best friend had been mad at her had been giving her a stomachache.) "I guess I'll just go practice by myself in the twins' bathroom now."

"Yvette, really," Reese said. "You don't have to practice in the bathroom. You can stay here."

"Actually, I *want* to," Yvette replied.

"You do? Why?" Gwen asked.

"The acoustics," Yvette said. "They're amazing in a bathroom! It's because of all that tile. Sounds bounce off tiles much better than regular walls. So you wind up getting a fuller sound."

"Cool!" O'Ryan said. "Now, let's get going!" And with her trumpet, she gave a mighty toot.

Hearing the trumpet sound, Sleepless (who had been asleep in the girls' bedroom) woke up and ran down the stairs.

"Hiya, Sleepless!" Gwen said, delighted to see the little puppy.

But even though Sleepless liked Gwen, he was not about to stop to say hello. He wanted to get as far away from the "music" as he could.

"All right, guys," Vanessa said. "According to the schedule, we start warming up with a little bebop improv."

"Bebop improv?" Gwen giggled. "Sounds like a dance move for a yellow jacket!" She took her drumsticks and started banging them against her knee, and then on her snare drum.

Reese, in turn, began strumming her bass.

"Nice, girls!" Vanessa said, with genuine excitement. "Okay, now I need my sax in there." She turned to Oki, who was sitting on the floor, braiding some of her mom's colorful scarves.

"Um, Oki, what are you *doing*?" Vanessa asked.

"I'm making some decorations for our microphone stands," Oki replied happily.

"But you're supposed to be *playing* now."

"Oh," Oki sighed. The idea of decorating the mic stands seemed a lot more exciting to her. But when she started to play, the sax added a nice sound to the drum and guitar, and everyone seemed pleased.

Gwen's drums sounded like this: *bah-bah-bah-bah-bah-bah-bah-bah.*

Reese's bass sounded like this: *bear-nere-nere.*

Oki's sax sounded like this: *dah-na…duh-na.*

"Cue, O'Ryan!" Vanessa said.

PPPFFFFFTTTTT, O'Ryan's trumpet blasted.

What a sound! There was just no way around the fact that O'Ryan sounded terrible on her trumpet.

"Um, O'Ryan," Vanessa said, "I think we have a *li*-ttle problem here. You know, because the trumpet is such a loud instrument, maybe—and I'm just spitballing here—it would help to be a *little* softer."

"Oh, okay!" O'Ryan whispered. "How's this?"

"Better. But now let your trumpet do the whispering!" Vanessa said. Then she added: "Gwen, Reese, and Oki—you guys take five!"

"Cool, and I know just what we can do with our five-minute break," Reese said. "We can make nachos in the kitchen!"

"Na-chos in the kitchen, my taste buds are itchin' for na-chos in the kitchen!" O'Ryan rapped.

As O'Ryan rhymed, Vanessa's eyes widened as an idea dawned on her. "You sound like you're really itching to sing, O'Ryan. So, go with me on this: How about becoming our new lead singer?"

"What?" O'Ryan asked. "I can't sing *and* play my trumpet at the same time."

"Exactly!" Vanessa replied. "I mean...it'd be way better to have a real live singer than to have to pretend to sing by lip-synching, anyway. So, would you consider singing *instead*? You'd really be helping us out."

O'Ryan thought about this for a second. (If she'd thought about it for any longer, she might have realized her trumpet-playing was being dissed. But she was so jazzed by the idea of singing, she accepted her new job right away.)

"I'd be happy to!" O'Ryan said excitedly.

"Super!" Vanessa replied. Then she yelled, "Hey, girls, come back! We're ready to practice together again!"

The girls put down their nacho fixings and ran in from the kitchen.

"Guess who's the new lead singer of our group?" O'Ryan said as they approached.

"Yvette?" Gwen and Reese asked hopefully.

"No, it's me!" O'Ryan said.

"Instead of playing the trumpet," Vanessa explained, "O'Ryan's going to sing for us."

"Oh," Reese exhaled, keeping the "uh-oh" to herself.

"Fantabulous!" Gwen replied.

Of course, Gwen had never heard O'Ryan sing.

"Okay, Groovies, take it from the top," Vanessa instructed. And when Vanessa hit the chick-a-chick-a-cha-cha chorus on her boom box, and O'Ryan began singing along, suddenly this "fantabulous" idea seemed a *little* off the mark...and a *lot* off key!

But, what O'Ryan lacked in vocal skill, she made up for in volume. She sang loudly and clearly...and it soon became clear to everyone that she was an even *worse* singer than trumpet player!

"What's going on?" Yvette said, as she came back into the living room. "I thought I heard Sleepless crying."

"Nope, that was me singing! I'm the new lead singer of the Groovy Group," O'Ryan said.

"Wow!" Yvette said. "That's...great." What else could she say? But then it hit her: Maybe she *could* help. "Hey, O'Ryan, my mom taught me a few neat tricks of the trade when I first started singing. If you want, I could teach them to you."

"That'd be supreme!" O'Ryan said.

"Well, cool, come on up to my 'office' then." Yvette giggled. She started walking back upstairs with O'Ryan at her heels. "You know, girls," Yvette called back to the others, "everyone's welcome!"

"Can we bring nachos?" Gwen asked.

"You not only *can*," Yvette replied, "but you SHOULD!"

So all the Groovies jammed into the upstairs bathroom, passing around the plate of nachos and making faces at one another in the mirror.

"Okay," Yvette said to O'Ryan, "why don't we take it from the top?"

As the two girls started singing together—just their two voices alone, without any music or instruments to back them up—they sounded strong and melodic.

"*Oh baby, baby!*" Yvette sang.

"Baby, baby!" O'Ryan echoed.

"You're my tamale. My little dolly. You're my big folly—" they sang together. "And do I looooooove you?...Prob'ly!"

And when they stopped singing, everyone applauded.

"Yippee!" Oki said. "That was awwwwesome!"

"And just imagine how much *better* O'Ryan will sound with even more practice!" Vanessa added.

Reese rolled her eyes. "Don't you think O'Ryan should rest her vocal chords or something?" she asked. "I mean, after all, we don't want her to lose her voice before the show." Actually, Reese thought, maybe that *wouldn't* be such a bad idea. To be honest, Reese was kind of worried. She really didn't want her sister to risk embarrassing herself in front of the whole school. And if O'Ryan embarrassed herself, Reese knew she'd feel embarrassed, too.

"Okay, let's break," Yvette agreed.

"Great!" Oki said. "In the meantime, you guys can try on some of the outfits I've put together."

The girls tried on silver pants and black tops, and danced around in them, making sure they could still do their moves.

"Excellent!" Vanessa said, checking off another

item on her clipboard list. "And now—"

"Please don't say we have more rehearsing," Reese begged.

"Okay, okay. No more practicing. At least not till tomorrow morning," Vanessa replied with a smile. "It's pizza time!"

"That's music to my ears!" Gwen shouted.

To go with their pizza, Vanessa whipped up a special tea with honey. "It coats the throat and soothes the scratches," Vanessa explained.

And as the Groovy Girls drank their tea and ate their 'za, they were happy. The talent show wasn't until next week, and the only talent they needed right now was the *Chick-a-chick-a-cha-cha* Chew!

"I think the inside of my belly's turned to jelly," Gwen told Vanessa the morning of the talent show.

"You have nothing to fear," Vanessa pronounced. "You've practiced like a crazy cat, you know your part colder than ice cream, *and* you're dressed beautiliciously. So don't worry."

"Didja have to say 'ice cream'?" Gwen frowned. "'Cause now on top of being nervous, I'm hungry, too!"

"Attention! Attention everyone!" Mr. Hornblower shouted. (In addition to being the music teacher, Mr. Hornblower also coordinated the talent show.) "Okay, people. I've randomly picked the acts from a hat, and this is the order in which you'll be performing."

Mike and Jay's magic act was up first. Yvette would be singing fifth, and, after nine other acts, the Groovy Group would be up last!

"How are you feeling?" Vanessa asked O'Ryan.

"Pretty good," O'Ryan said, sipping some honey-lemon water Vanessa had prepared for her.

Truthfully, O'Ryan was a little nervous. Now that the talent show was here, she wasn't feeling so fine about being the lead singer. And she suddenly wished the Groovies would be doing something more like a soccer demonstration instead, because soccer was something she knew how to do well.

"The auditorium doors will be opening for the audience any moment now!" Mr. Hornblower said.

"Groovy Group, hallway please!" Oki called out.

The girls followed Oki into the hallway, where she tugged at their purple, black, and silver tops and pants, making sure everything sat just right.

"Oki," Vanessa said, as she inspected the troupe, "you did a great job with our girls!"

"Thank you." Oki curtsied.

———

"Good morning and welcome to the school talent show," Mr. Hornblower's voice boomed through the speakers. "We have some amazingly talented performers today from the third, fourth, and fifth grades. And at the end of the show, the student council members and I will rank the acts. The top three finishers will go to the district-wide talent show next month."

When the girls heard this, another wave of excitement and nerves rolled over them.

"So now," Mr. Hornblower said, "without any further delay, let's get this show on the road!"

When Mr. Hornblower introduced Mike and

Jay, the girls ran to the side of the stage to watch.

Much to the girls' surprise, the boys *did* manage to pull off a few neat card tricks, like "Knee Jack Reaction," "Now You See It, Now You're Seeing It Double," and "Turn that U on Your Report Card into an O!" (True, that last one wasn't very hard, but it *could* be very useful.)

As the boys finished and the audience clapped, Mr. Hornblower reminded students, "Don't try that last trick at home!"

Acts two, three, and four passed like a blur for the girls backstage, and Yvette, who had been warming up her voice in the bathroom, came out just before her name was called.

"Are you nervous?" O'Ryan asked her.

"Not really," Yvette replied. "Just excited."

And when she was announced, Yvette strode out to center stage. She took hold of the microphone and, as soon as the music started, she began belting out her tune.

Yvette hit the high notes with grace, the low notes with heart, and she moved across the stage like she owned it.

"Just like a flower
Blooming in spring,
You gave me power
Made my soul sing.

And when I felt lonely,
You understood.
You're my one and only.
You make me feel so good."

When she finished, the audience exploded in applause, and the Groovies rushed to congratulate her backstage.

As each act passed, the Groovy Group waited for their turn, and it felt like hours. But then finally, when the girls heard Mr. Hornblower say, "Our last act—" Vanessa ran out onstage.

"Ladies and gentlemen, boys and girls, STAND UP!" Vanessa commanded. "'Cause this final act is gonna rock your socks off! And now, here they are...the Groovy Girls Group!"

As Vanessa made her introduction, Gwen, Reese, Oki, and O'Ryan were taking their positions behind the curtain.

Then, from her spot behind the drum set, Gwen yelled, "ONE, TWO," and started rat-a-tat tapping the intro. Reese joined in a moment later on her bass, then cued Oki on her sax. After the opening chorus, O'Ryan was supposed to start on vocals.

But when O'Ryan looked out into the audience and saw the whole school sitting in front of her— the hundreds of eyes staring and the hundreds of ears listening—a shudder ran through her body!

Her knees locked.

Her throat closed.

And she froze!

Froze like an ice cube in Antarctica.

Reese looked at her sister worriedly, wondering how she could help.

Oki and Gwen shared a nervous look.

What were they going to do?!

Then the girls saw something truly beautiful.

Something stunningly superb.

It was Yvette, striding out onstage, microphone in hand. She linked arms with O'Ryan and started singing:

> *"Oh baby, yooooooouuuuuuuuu,*
> *You are my morning breeze*
> *You solve my mysteries*
> *You cure my heart disease."*

With her nerves melting at the sight and sound of her friend, O'Ryan found her voice again, and the harmony she created with Yvette filled the auditorium.

Yvette turned to look at Gwen, Reese, and Oki, and they all smiled back, playing louder and better than they ever had before!

"Oh baby, youuuuuuuuu!!!" the Groovies roared.

The girls kept rocking and before they knew it, it was time for the final sweeping chorus.

 "Chick-a-chick-a-cha-cha
Chick-a-chick-a-cha-cha
Chick-a-chick-a-cha-cha-cha!"

When the music stopped, the clapping started and the auditorium roared with applause. The Groovy Girls Group stepped forward and each of

its members took a big bow, singly at first, and then again all together.

When the girls walked offstage, Vanessa ran up to Yvette and threw her arms around her.

"Yvette," Vanessa said, "you rock!"

"Thanks," Yvette replied. "But it was a great team effort, you know?"

"It sure was," Reese nodded. "And you were our MVP!"

Mr. Hornblower jogged back out onstage a moment later, congratulating all the performers and telling the audience he'd have the results for the top three finishers shortly.

All the acts gathered on the wings of the stage, waiting to hear the final results. Mike and Jay sauntered up to Gwen.

"You guys were good," Mike said.

"Thanks!" Gwen replied, surprised that Mike was actually being nice to her. "And your magic act was really cool, too."

"True," Mike replied. "So, it's too bad you guys aren't going to go to the district finals with us."

Gwen screwed up her face—why had she let herself think Mike was going

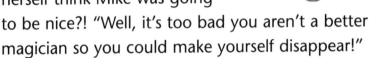

to be nice?! "Well, it's too bad you aren't a better magician so you could make yourself disappear!"

Vanessa quickly moved Gwen away from Mike before drumsticks started flying.

"Okay!" Mr. Hornblower said, running back out onstage. "I now hold the names of the three acts who will be representing our school in the district-wide finals!"

The girls looked at one another excitedly, hoping their names would be called. O'Ryan took Reese's hand, and they shared one of those special twin moments where they both thought, *I'm so glad you're here with me.*

"Our third place contestant won points for originality, delivery, and passion, earning him a spot in the district finals. Congratulations, Paul, on your dramatic performance of 'Casey at the Bat.'"

The audience clapped wildly. Popular Paul

was a crowd favorite. (Even if his act was weird!)

The Groovies looked at one another. Cool, spots number two and one were left, and either would work just fine for them and Yvette!

"Our judges were also awed and impressed by Karly and Lisa's dance performance, earning them the second spot at districts!"

Karly and Lisa jumped up and down as the Groovy Girls' smiles began to drop. There was only one spot left....

"And our highest scorer, an act we'll all be proud to have representing us in the district finals, is..."

Mr. Hornblower paused and smiled.

All the girls were going koo-koo-ka-razy!

"...Yvette! Congratulations!"

Yvette beamed.

And then, so did all the other Groovy Girls. They really were thrilled for their friend.

But, even though they were happy for Yvette, in truth they were also a little sad for themselves.

And it was okay to feel disappointed, since they'd worked so hard. But as soon as Oki pointed out that a victory for one of them was really a victory for all of them, they started feeling better again.

Mr. Hornblower walked past the girls a moment later. "I just want you to know the Groovy Girls Group came in a very close fourth place," he said.

"Thanks," Vanessa replied. "Nice to know, even if it doesn't really matter."

Wait a sec, Yvette thought, a big, glorious idea sprouting in her mind like a sunflower. *Maybe it can matter!*

She ran up to Mr. Hornblower and whispered something to him. He scratched his head, then put out his hands as if to say, "why not?" Yvette smiled at him winningly, then ran back to the group.

"Guess what I just found out?" she said to her friends.

"What?"

"If one of the top three acts can't perform, it means you guys go to district finals."

"Yeah," Vanessa said. "But what's the chance of that happening?"

"Pretty good, actually," Yvette said and smiled. "Because I just told Mr. Hornblower I can't perform without the Groovy Girls Group behind me."

"Yvette," Vanessa said, "you can't give up your—"

"Vanessa," her best friend replied, "I'm not just

doing this for them, I'm doing this for me, too."

"What do you mean? You don't need the Groovy Girls to sound great."

"That's true," Yvette replied, "but I've realized I'm even *better* when my friends are around me. And I have more fun. So what do you say, girls?" Yvette asked. "Will you help me out by playing with me in districts?"

This was not a question the girls needed to be asked twice.

"*Oh baby, yoooooooouuuuuuuuuuu!*" they all started singing in response, and they took Yvette into a tight group hug.

"I'm gonna take that as a yes!" Yvette said, giggling.

"What a great day!" Vanessa exclaimed. Then, turning back to the Groovies, she said, "And I expect the fun to continue at practice later this afternoon, this weekend, and every day till districts!"

The Groovy Group all groaned in response. But it still made for a very happy, musical sound!

Groovy Girls™
sleepover handbook

BE AN OVERNIGHT SENSATION!
Throw your own **TALENT SHOW SLEEPOVER!**

Jazz Up Your
JAM SESSIONS
with Instant Musical Instruments

SWINGIN' SNACKS
Fruit Kabobs, Slushies, Smoothies, and More!

Contents

Text by Julia Marsden
Illustrations by Yancey Labat, Bill Alger, Kurt Marquart

I'm heading back to rehearsal with the Groovies in a few minutes, but first I want to fill you in on all our latest rockin' and rollin'! For the school talent show, we're forming a rock band—and you'll either think we're *sing*-sational or filled with musical madness. (How we sound all depends on whether you're onstage with us—or in the audience, I suppose.)

Ready for your own moment in the spotlight? Then read on!

The jammin' begins with the pizzaz-ziest party ever: A Talent Show Sleepover! Pages 4–5 are filled with glitzy and glammy party ideas, solo acts for the stage (ahem, my specialty!), and a hip-hoppin' song-and-dance competition! To dazzle like a star, onstage or off, turn to page 6 for ideas on how to add some serious sparkle to your stage style or—for sleepover fun—to jazz up your jammies. Before you know it, you'll be a diva designer, just like Oki!

Ready to take five? When you need a rehearsal time-out, turn to page 11 for some power-packed peanut butter balls and yummy kabobs. And for soothing your throat after lots of singing, acting, or stage managing, try the lemon-and-honey drinks on pages 12–13. They're do-re-mi fab!

With all this talent-show talk, you may be wondering just what kind of star you are. Whether you're a musical master or a musical deee-zaster, check out pages 8–9 for all kinds of terrific ways you can strut your stuff—from cooking to creative writing!

Just remember—whichever way you choose to shine, you'll always be a superstar!

Till next time, groovy girl—rock on!

Love ya lots,
Yvette

Set the Stage for a
TALENT SHOW SLEEPOVER

What could be better than a sleepover that gives each of your guests a chance to shine? Host a Talent Show Sleepover for your friends—and watch all the stars come out at night!

Here are the extras every girl should bring:

♪ A flashlight for spotlighting great performances!

♪ Props she may need for her solo act

♪ An old T-shirt for pizzaz-zing up her wardrobe (See page 9 for a couple of cute T-shirt designs.)

♪ Some favorite CDs or tapes

♪ A hairbrush for styling her strands—and to double as a microphone

♪ Comfy jammies to wear during rehearsals and when relaxing backstage

♪ A costume change for offstage acts (that is, a change of clothes for the next morning)

Here's what to do:

♪ Prepare a program. It can be a single sheet of paper listing the performances and each performer's name in the order they will appear, or you can create something fancier with cover art, performer bios, and good-luck messages from family and friends.

♪ Give out a Star Award (a roll of Starburst® candy, for example) to all performers in such categories as Laugh-Out-Loud Performance, Incredibly Inspired, and Grand Glam.

TALENT SHOW PROGRAM

4

10 Awesome Acts
When the spotlight's on you, why not...

♫ sing a song.

♪ do a dance.

♫ tell jokes.

♪ perform a magic trick.

♫ impersonate a pal or a fave celeb.

♫ act a role from a play.

♪ perform a tumbling or gymnastics routine.

♫ draw a cartoon or caricature.

♪ play a musical instrument.

♫ whip up one of your fave snacks or desserts in front of—and for—your audience.

Sing It, Girls!
Get set for a swingin', singin', dancin' competition!

1. Divide into two teams of two to six players each.

2. Have both teams grab a boom box and some favorite CDs or tapes. Each team should decide on one song to perform.

3. Choreograph a dance routine together. Have each team member add a dance move until the routine is complete.

4. Rehearse in separate areas so the teams won't be influenced by each other.

5. Have both teams introduce their group, the individual performers, and the song they will be performing.

6. For added fun, change the lyrics to a favorite song by replacing a few words or by adding someone's name to the mix, or, if you want to focus on your stage presence, lip-synch the whole song from start to finish.

7. Capture your world-premier performances using a video or digital camera.

5

WINNING LOOKS from the
Wardrobe Department

Take your pick!
Pizzaz-zy pajamas, serious sparkle, and hot hairstyles can all add to your stage presence. Here are a bunch of ideas for dazzling divas!

Jammin' Jammies

Give your PJs some performance-worthy pizzazz!

* Scrunch up the sleeves of your pajama top and wear the top open over a cute camisole.

* Roll the hems of your pajama bottoms to create capri-length cuffs.

* Tie a scarf or wide ribbon around your waist as a belt.

* Slide into some stylish slippers or fancy flip-flops (like the kind that has a big flower between the toes) before you take to the stage.

Star Power

Sparkle for your stage performance!

* Add body glitter to your cheeks or hair.

* Accessorize with stick-on jewelry and rhinestones.

* Paint your fingernails using glitter or glow-in-the-dark nail polish.

Happening Hairstyles

Show off your creative talents with a stylin' hairdo!

* Make a high ponytail and secure it with a rockin' ribbon scrunchie that you make by looping and knotting 9-inch strands of colorful ribbon onto an elastic hair band.

* Create tiny braids all over your head and add a colorful rubber band or tiny barrette to the end of each.

6

Solo Solutions and TALENT TIPS

Ready for a solo act? Feeling a little jealous of a superstar sib? Then read on for some tips on how to shine in your own spotlight!

Star Struck

I want to perform solo in the school talent show but my friends want me to be part of their act. I'd like to put on a great performance and I'm afraid that appearing onstage with them might not give me the chance to show off my talent. What should I do?

Let your friends know that you're really excited about performing on your own. Ask them what their performance will be all about and share with them your onstage act, too. Maybe there's a way you can showcase your individual talent while performing with the group. Yvette can definitely give a sizzling solo, but she can also dazzle alongside the other Groovies. Even if you decide to take to the stage alone, you can still help out by giving fab feedback or awesome advice.

Terrific Talents

My sister is great at sports and gets lots of attention because of it. Sometimes I get kind of jealous. I wish I could be really good at sports, too. What should I do?

Everyone has special abilities—one of your sister's happens to be sports. Rather than comparing yourself to her and focusing on how great she is at all things athletic, take some time to tune into the things you enjoy and excel at. Then dive into those activities with extra enthusiasm. Redirect your focus back on the things you do best, and you'll discover how good it feels to tap into your own unique talents! (To explore different kinds of talents and interests, check out pages 8–9!) And if you still would like to focus on improving your game in the sports department, the great news is you've got a cool coach living right under your own roof!

Shining Star!

How do you shimmer and sparkle? Check out all the different ways you can be a creative star...

Are You a Visual Artist?

If you love to take a close look at things and are into all the cool details, you've got a visual vibe.

Ways to express yourself: Try your hand at painting or pottery. Take a trip to an art museum or gallery. Grab a sketchbook and start drawing, or shoot a roll of film throughout the day to see what your life looks like in pictures.

Are You a Musical Artist?

If the idea of appearing onstage with a microphone in hand and a backup band makes your heart skip a beat, you've got the music in you.

Ways to express yourself: Sing your favorite tunes into a tape recorder (you can play a CD in the background for backup) and get jammin' with your friends during a Talent Show Sleepover (see pages 4–5)!

Are You a Literary Artist?

When you visit a library, bookstore, or magazine stand, you usually end up wondering where all the time went. And your friends often tell you that you have an amazing way with words.

Ways to express yourself: Put pen to paper by creating a continuing story that you add to each day. You can also try exchanging a writing journal with a friend, so you can both contribute to a story—or even share your own stories with each other.

Are You a Culinary Artist?

You like to whip up winning recipes and are known for inviting your friends over for full-on food-a-thons!

Ways to express yourself: Stage a cake-decorating contest, or set up a cookie exchange with your pals—everyone shows up with a batch of cookie creations to share and trade, so each person ends up with a varied selection of edible offerings!

Are You a Dramatic Artist?

If you're all about imagining yourself giving an acceptance speech at the Academy Awards®, odds are you often play the part of a pure performer.

Ways to express yourself: Audition for a part in a theater production and get ready to demonstrate your dramatic flair in front of a live audience! You can also star in a dance performance, or tumble through a gymnastics routine.

Are You a Fashion Artist?

So, like Oki, you have a passion for fashion! Your outfits and accessories are all about showing off your original sense of style.

Ways to express yourself: Put on a fashion show with some friends, design fab T-shirts, or visit a fabric shop for some funky fabric swatches you can add to an outfit.

Curtain Call CLUES

If you want to ease those onstage
(and backstage) jitters, here are some ways to
prepare for your performance before all eyes are on you!

Be Clear

Whether you'll be singing a song, delivering a speech, or telling a few jokes, you'll want to make things clear and pump up the volume. To practice speaking clearly, try a few tongue twisters. They'll help you focus on getting each syllable of each word you say right.

Try saying these twisters as quickly and clearly as you can:

* **She sells seashells down by the seashore.**

* **How much wood would a woodchuck chuck if a woodchuck could chuck wood?**

* **Peter Piper picked a peck of pickled peppers.**

SAY GOOD-BYE TO STAGE FRIGHT

The butterflies in your stomach right before a performance can feel more like buzzards. And that's completely normal. The adrenaline in your body makes you feel nervous and excited. So, if you're feeling all aflutter, here are some ways to get a grip!

* Remind yourself that you've rehearsed well and that the audience is on your side. (Picturing them in their underwear can also help you put yourself at ease!)

* Before going onstage, do some deep breathing, or loosen up by letting your whole body feel completely floppy and relaxed.

* If you'll be performing onstage, the bright lights can block your view of the audience, so tell yourself that you're just rehearsing.

* If you'll be standing up in class, pick a friendly face in the room and focus your attention on her, rather than the whole group.

INSTANT ENERGY TREATS
and Thirst Quenchers

Refuel during rehearsals with these protein-packed snacks!

Peanut Butter Power Balls

(Makes about 25 balls)

Ingredients:

1 cup peanut butter or your favorite nut butter

1 cup honey

2 cups instant dry milk powder (in the baking supply aisle of your grocery store)

1 cup coconut flakes (optional)

Utensils: Measuring cups, measuring spoon, large mixing bowl, serving plate

What You Do:

1. Measure the peanut butter, honey, and dry milk into a large mixing bowl and knead into dough.

2. Scoop a tablespoon of dough and roll it into a ball. Repeat until all the dough has been rolled into balls.

3. If you want, roll the balls in coconut flakes.

4. Place on a plate and chill in the fridge until ready to serve.

Cool Kabobs *(Makes about 8 kabobs)*

Ingredients:

Choice Cheeses

Mozzarella cubes

Monterey Jack cubes

Cheddar cubes

Colby cubes

Swiss cubes

Fab Fruits

1 apple, sliced

1 pear, sliced

1 banana, peeled and sliced

Seedless grapes

1 can of pineapple chunks

Utensils: Chopsticks or skewers, serving plate

What You Do:

1. Skewer any of the choice cheeses or fab fruits onto chopsticks or skewers. (If you're using chopsticks, make sure to cut big cubes of cheeses and large chunks of fruit, so they won't split when you skewer them.)

2. Place the skewers on a plate and serve.

Sweet-as-Honey
LEMON AID

For a quick cool down, or to soothe an over-used throat, try a scrumptious smoothie or a slurp-a-licious slush! Then win over your audience, just like the Groovy Girls do, by putting on a crowd-pleasing performance!

Lemonade Fizz *(Makes 1 serving)*

Ingredients:

¹/₂ cup lemonade
(You can buy a carton of pre-made lemonade, or you can make lemonade from concentrate.)

¹/₂ cup lemon-lime soda or sparkling lemon-flavored water

Utensils: Measuring cup

What You Do:

1. Pour the lemonade into a tall glass.

2. Fill the glass to the top with lemon-lime soda or sparkling lemon-flavored water.

Groovy Smoothie *(Makes 1 serving)*

Ingredients:

¹/₂ banana, peeled and sliced

¹/₂ cup lemon yogurt (or any flavored yogurt of your choice)

1 teaspoon honey

About 5 ice cubes

Utensils: Butter knife, measuring cup, measuring spoon, blender

What You Do:

1. Put all the ingredients in a blender.

2. Ask an adult to blend until smooth.

3. Pour into a tall glass.

Super-Citrusy Energizer *(Makes 1 serving)*

Ingredients:

$^1/_2$ cup frozen lemon yogurt
(You can buy frozen yogurt, or you can freeze a small container of yogurt.)

1 cup orange juice

$^1/_2$ teaspoon freshly squeezed lemon juice (optional)

Utensils: Measuring cups, measuring spoon, blender

What You Do:

1. Put the frozen yogurt and juice into a blender.

2. Ask an adult to blend until smooth.

3. Pour into a tall glass.

4. Taste, and add the lemon juice if the drink is too sweet.

Strawberry Lemonade Slush *(Makes 2 servings)*

Ingredients:

About 20 strawberries, with stems removed and cleaned
(You can also use frozen strawberries, blueberries, or raspberries.)

$^1/_2$ cup lemonade
(You can buy a carton of pre-made lemonade, or you can make lemonade from concentrate.)

1 teaspoon honey

About 10 ice cubes

Utensils: Measuring cup, measuring spoon, blender

What You Do:

1. Put the ingredients into a blender.

2. Ask an adult to blend until slushy.

3. Pour the slush into glasses.

Shake, Rattle, and Roll

Add some serious sound to your performances by creating percussion instruments from ordinary objects you find around the house!

Get into the **rhythm...**

with a *guiro* (WE-row), an instrument that's all about rubbing up some sound!

To make a water-bottle guiro: Choose an empty plastic water bottle that has ridges on the outside. To make noise, rub the edges using a pencil, wooden spoon, or chopstick.

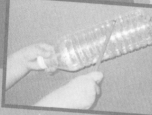

Dance to the beat of a **different drum!**

To make a coffee-can steel drum: Use the bottom of an empty coffee can as your drum. Play your drum by using pencils or chopsticks.

To make a water-cooler bass drum: Hold an empty 5-gallon water-cooler jug under one arm. Strike the bottom of the jug with a wooden spoon or the palm of your hand.

Really shake **things up!**

Make some *maracas* (muh-RAH-kuhs) by using film canisters or empty vitamin containers (be sure to ask a parent before you empty out all those vitamins!). Fill the canisters or containers with some dried rice, macaroni, or beans. Close the lids and make sure they're secure. Beans or macaroni will create a loud rattle. Rice will create a softer swishing sound.

rice

pasta

beans

For **Pizzaz-zier** Playing

Jazz up your instruments by covering them with construction paper, adding some stickers, or wrapping sections with colorful ribbon.

Set the room **abuzz!**

To make a cardboard tube kazoo:

Attach a square of waxed paper to one end of a cardboard tube (from a paper towel or toilet paper roll) with a rubber band. Make sure the square of waxed paper is big enough to wrap around the tube's edge, so you can keep it in place with the rubber band. With a pencil, punch two or three holes (about an inch apart) on the side of the tube. To play the kazoo, place the uncovered end of the tube in your mouth, breathe in through your nose, and hum out through your mouth. As you hum into the tube, cover the holes with your fingers to create different tones.

To make a straw kazoo:

Use your teeth to flatten one end of a drinking straw. With a pair of scissors, snip the flattened end into a small V. To play the kazoo, place the V end in your mouth, press your lips together, and blow.

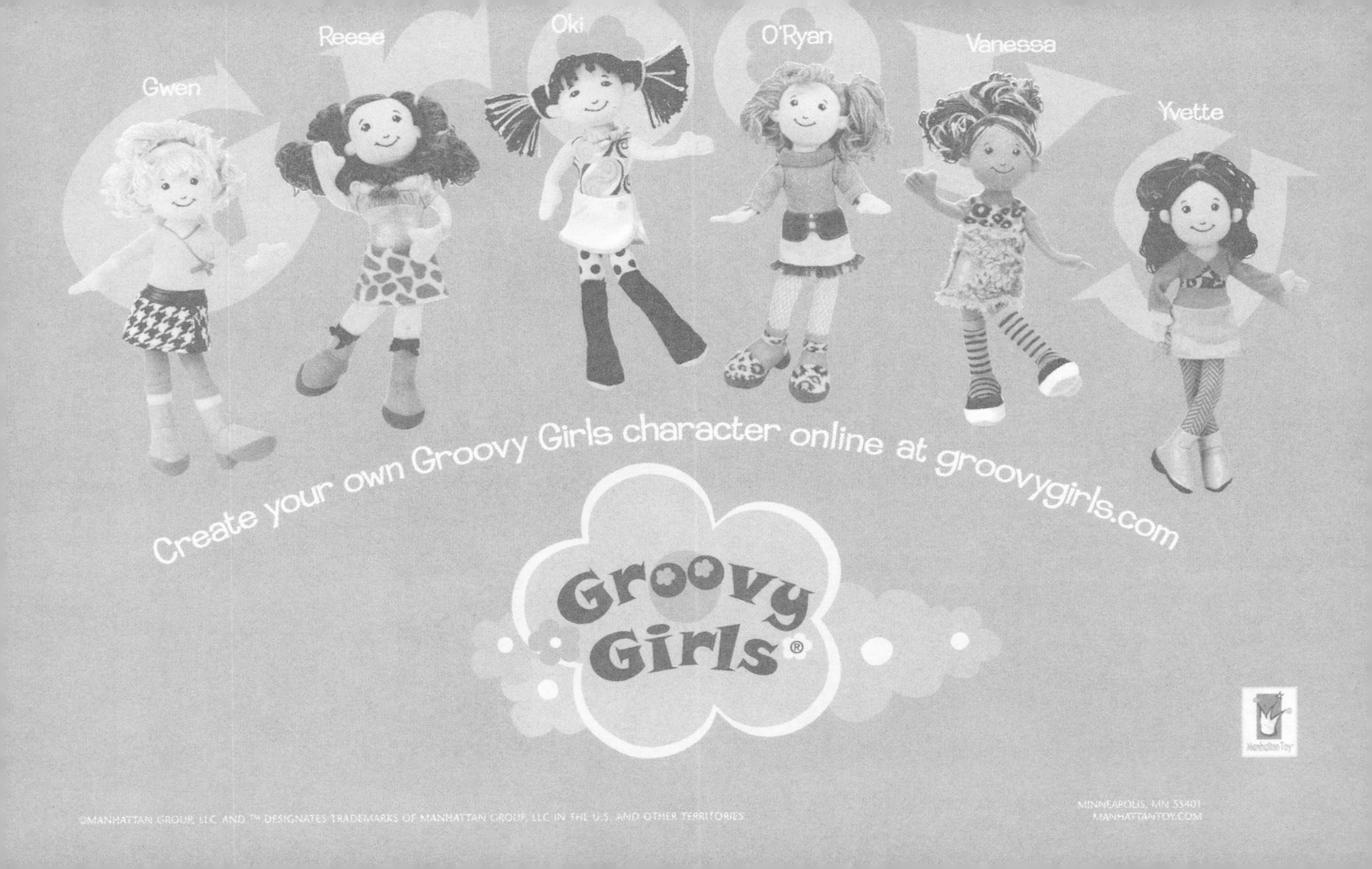

Gwen
Reese
Oki
O'Ryan
Vanessa
Yvette
Create your own Groovy Girls character online at groovygirls.com
Groovy Girls®
©MANHATTAN GROUP, LLC AND ™ DESIGNATES TRADEMARKS OF MANHATTAN GROUP, LLC IN THE U.S. AND OTHER TERRITORIES
MINNEAPOLIS, MN 55401
MANHATTANTOY.COM